THE SQUIRRELS
WHO SQUABBLED

For Robbie – Bestest sharer of everything
in life (except chips) – R B

For our dear little Lola,
aka the Double Chinnais Guru.
Welcome to the World – J F

ORCHARD BOOKS
First published in Great Britain in hardback in 2017
by The Watts Publishing Group
This edition first published in 2018

1 3 5 7 9 10 8 6 4 2

Text © Rachel Bright, 2017
Illustrations © Jim Field, 2017

A CIP catalogue record for this book is available from the British Library

978 1 40834 047 9

Printed and bound in China

MIX
Paper from
responsible sources
FSC
www.fsc.org   FSC® C104740

Orchard Books, an imprint of Hachette Children's Group
Part of The Watts Publishing Group Limited
Carmelite House,
50 Victoria Embankment,
London EC4Y 0DZ
An Hachette UK Company
www.hachette.co.uk
www.hachettechildrens.co.uk

THE SQUIRRELS
WHO SQUABBLED

Rachel
BRIGHT

Jim
FIELD

ORCHARD

In a towering forest, where summer had been,
The cool air bit fresh and the mosses grew green.
And as autumn edged in and the sky raged red,
The sleepiest creatures got ready for bed.

While, up in a tree,

swung a flighty young squirrel,

Who everyone knew as

'Spontaneous Cyril'.

Now, most foresty folk
had seen to their needs,
Through the plentiful months
of mushrooms and seeds.

They'd built up their stores
so they'd all be well fed
Through the frosting of winter
that glittered ahead.

But Cyril, he lived in the
NOW and the **HERE**.
He'd adventured and partied
his way through the year.

So his cupboard was empty,
his hollow was bare.

He hadn't a mouthful of
food **ANYWHERE**.

BUT WAIT! What was that?
Over there! Take a look!
A single lone pine-cone,
wedged in a nook!
He squealed with delight —
and for very good reason . . .

For inside were the

Very.

Last.

Nuts.

Of.

The.

Season.

BUT . . . Cyril wasn't alone.
There were more hungry eyes.
Yes, 'Plan-Ahead Bruce'
had his sights on the prize.

Though he'd gathered a mountain
of bounty, hard-fought,
Bruce was convinced
he was ONE PINE CONE SHORT.

'I simply MUST have it!'
he wistfully cried,
As he dreamt of the fresh,
juicy pine-nuts inside.

So as Cyril set off
on his way to the ground,
Bruce, he was also
LAST-PINE-CONE-bound!

They sprinted and scurried —
with no time to gamble,
They scratched at the bark
in their scampering scramble.

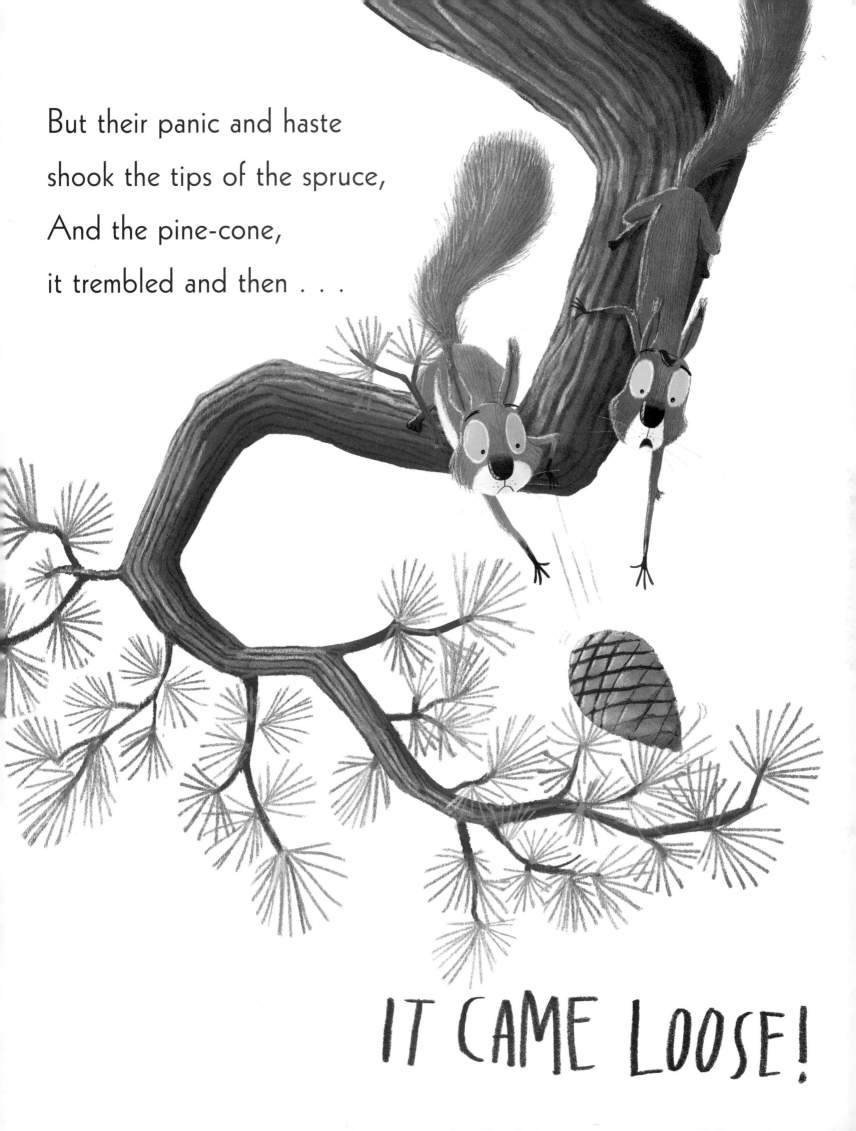

But their panic and haste
shook the tips of the spruce,
And the pine-cone,
it trembled and then . . .

IT CAME LOOSE!

Both squirrels gave
chase at a lightning pace.
This was the start of a
wild nutty race . . .

'It's mine!' shouted Cyril.

'No, mine!' hollered Bruce . . .

'You don't stand a chance!
Give up! It's no use!'

'I'm **HUNGRY!**' cried Cyril.
'This cone is **NOT** yours!'

'Stay back!' shouted Bruce.
'This cone's for **MY** stores!'

It BOINGED over bushes . . . .

and flew through the air.

It **BINGED** on the nose of a slumbering bear!

It **BOUNCED** over boulders then came to a . . .

STOP.

Then teetered
and wobbled
and quivered
and . . .

PLOP!

Both squirrels followed.
Oh! The water was fast!
Would they learn that they needed
each other at last?

But EACH was intent
on how HE could win,
So they didn't quite notice
A BIRD SWEEPING IN!

Cyril and Bruce,

they watched in dismay,

As their cone disappeared up

up . . . UP . . . and AWAY!

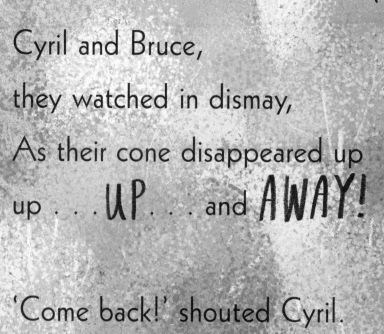

'Come back!' shouted Cyril.

'They're our nuts!' exclaimed Bruce.

But all hope was gone.

It was simply no use.

And meanwhile they drifted
right up to the ledge.
Greed, it was driving them . . .

OVER THE EDGE.

Cyril and Bruce,
they had taken a fall.

They were paying the price
for wanting it all.

They'd squandered their chances
to team up and share.

Would their nutty young hopes
simply end in despair?

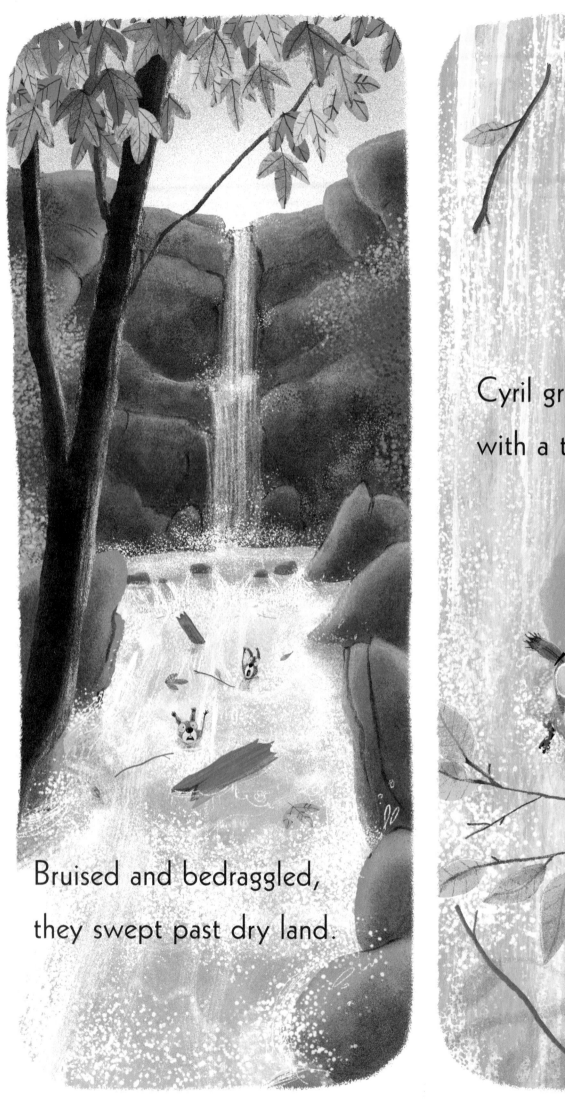

Bruised and bedraggled,
they swept past dry land.

Cyril grabbed at a branch
with a trembling hand.

Catching Bruce with
the other, he heaved
and he huffed . . .

And dragged him to safety,
with panting and puffs.

They stared at the sky,
quite lost in deep thought,
Until Bruce looked at
Cyril and . . .

Let out a **SNORT.**

'How silly we are!'
he proclaimed, all a-jiggle.
'How greedy I've been!'
spluttered Bruce with a giggle.

'We shall change from today.
May the squabbling cease.
We should celebrate — seeing
we're both in one piece!'

From that day and forward,
they made a great pair.
They would gather together
and found they COULD share.

Yes, Cyril and Bruce,
they knew in the end . . .

The **BEST** thing to share is
a laugh with your friend.